Feel Like Eggs?

In loving memory of
Roger Goodman

Copyright © 2021 by Jeff Goodman. All rights reserved

Editor: Lorraine Wadman
Illustrator: Gabriella Urbina
Creative Director and Designer: Susan Shankin

No part of this book may be reproduced or transmitted in any form or by any means, electronic or mechanical, including photocopying, recording, or by an information storage and retrieval system—except by a reviewer who may quote brief passages in a review to be printed in a magazine, newspaper, or on the web—without permission in writing from the publisher. For permission requests, email the publisher at: susan@precocitypress.com

ISBN: 978-1-7352921-8-2

Library of Congress Control Number: 2020924397

Published by Precocity Press
Venice, CA 90291

First edition. Printed and bound in the United States of America

Feel Like Eggs?

Written by Jeff Goodman
Illustrated by Gabriella Urbina

PRECOCITY PRESS

A dozen eggs are chilling
In a carton on the shelf.
They all have special qualities
That fit inside one self.

All together in the fridge,
The dozen eggs have wishes
To express their different feelings
Through a wide array of dishes.

This egg has an outlook
That's positive all day.

Its sunny side is up because
Its joy is on display!

This egg is really silly;

It loves to laugh and giggle.

Its jokes go over easy

And make its insides wiggle!

This egg is hard boiled;
It wears its outer shell.
It needs to be protected
Or else it won't do well!

This egg is slightly nervous;

It's hiding in a salad.

Mayo helps to mask it

But its feeling is still valid.

This egg is awfully wacky;
It's broken, mixed, and stirred.
Its thoughts are scrambled totally
So it almost seems absurd!

This egg is overconfident;

It feels the need to boast.

It smothers bread and sizzles

As it turns into French toast!

This egg is soft and sensitive
When carelessly approached.
But when it's treated nicely,
It is gloriously poached!

This egg is slightly naughty;

It tends to mess around.

Its insides have been deviled

So mischief may abound.

This egg is quite surprised at how
An omelet comes about.
Meats and veggies startle it
And now it's flipping out!

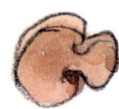

This egg is feeling angry;
It fumes when it's provoked.
It needs some time to let off steam
After being grilled and smoked!

This egg has fallen in a hole
And now it's feeling down.
There's sadness in its teary eyes
And sorrow in its frown.

This egg is kind and tender;

It's baked well in an oven.

It cares so much, it hugs the pan

And offers lots of lovin'!

"Feel like eggs?" you might be asked.

The carton's filled with choices.

The eggs can share their feelings

In different kinds of voices.

Sometimes it is hard to know

Which feeling's in your heart.

So open up your carton and

The eggs will help you start!

Starting with Editor's Corner exercises in third grade, **Jeff Goodman** has long found joy in the magic of the written word. Drawn to the world of children's literature for its unique ability to impart life lessons, Jeff wrote *Feel Like Eggs?* to help kids understand and express the feelings they experience in their daily lives.

As an award-winning journalist and school communications specialist, Jeff has written extensively about education, child development, and social-emotional learning. He currently works in communications at UCLA.

An alumnus of UC Berkeley, Jeff lives in Los Angeles with his wife and daughter. He enjoys playing basketball, spending time at the beach, solving crossword puzzles, and volunteering with childhood literacy organizations. Learn more about Jeff at jeffgoodmanauthor.com.

Gabriella Urbina is from Sweden, a country where 400,000 wild moose are roaming free in the woods. There, close to the Arctic Circle, Gabriella grew up an only child among trolls, elves, and other mystical forest creatures and developed an affection for dreaming, drawing, and reading, which earned her a degree in Fine Art and, later, a job within digital media. After 25 years of freezing cold winters Gabriella moved to the sunny beaches of California and started working as an artist for Hollywood movies.

For the last five years Gabriella has been working in the children's picture book industry as a writer and illustrator and is now living in Venice Beach with her family. The Urbina family consumes up to three cartons of eggs per week, mostly on scrambled or soft boiled eggs depending on the mood of the day.

Made in the USA
Las Vegas, NV
08 December 2020